Curious George ®

THREE TALES FOR A WINTER'S NIGHT

For information about permission to reproduce selections from this book, write to Permissions, Houghton Mifflin Harcourt Publishing Company, 215 Park Avenue South, New York, New York 10003.

ISBN: 978-0-547-83936-3

Design by Afsoon Razavi
www.hmhbooks.com

Printed in China/ LEO 10 9 8 7 6 5 4 3 2 1
4500373386

Houghton Mifflin Harcourt • Boston New York

Curious George®
The Surprise Gift

Adaptation by Erica Zappy
Based on the TV series teleplay written by Raye Lankford

George was a good little monkey and always very curious. This afternoon George was curious about a large box his friend was bringing home. A large box meant a large gift!

"Sorry, George," said his friend, setting the gift on the table. "This present's not for you. It's for Professor Wiseman's birthday. She'll open it at dinner tonight."

George was disappointed. Dinner was hours away. He wanted to know what was under the wrapping paper right now.

It was lucky George didn't have much time to think about the present. His friend needed help preparing Professor Wiseman's birthday dinner.

"Here is something to unwrap," said his friend. "Peel this orange to get to the good stuff." George took the rind off—SQUIRT! The orange peel had kept the sweet juice inside.

George realized
there was a lot of food in
the kitchen that could be
unwrapped! Bananas, apples,
cheese, even an onion—stinky!
Soon George had unwrapped many
yummy things. Maybe too many . . .
But he still didn't know what was under the wrapping
paper of the gift.

Before George could let his curiosity get the best of him, his friend sent him to the department store to pick up his new suit.

At the store, George encountered many presents. There were gift boxes everywhere he looked, all brightly colored and too tempting for one little monkey to resist.

George unwrapped a box, but there was nothing interesting to him inside.

In the window display,
there were more gift boxes.
Strangely enough, the boxes
had nothing at all inside. They
were used for decoration . . .
though not anymore!
   Now George couldn't wait
to help unwrap the present
at home. He was sure it would
have *something* inside. George
hurried to finish his errand.

When George got home, the present was nowhere to be found! The man with the yellow hat had wisely hidden it from his curious little monkey. Did that stop George?

George looked under the table for the surprise gift. Then he went to check the bedrooms and the bathroom.

In the bathroom George noticed that the walls were covered in wrapping paper. George scratched. He peeled. He unwrapped. What did George find after all the unwrapping?

A wall! Unlike presents and fruit, nothing especially good was hiding underneath.

Luckily there was still something left to unwrap that promised something very nice (and very big) inside! It was time for Professor Wiseman to open her birthday gift.

   With George's help she unwrapped and unwrapped and unwrapped.

Inside the big box was a small gift. "I never thought a present like this would be in such a big box," she said. The man with the yellow hat had wrapped it up so that she would have a harder time guessing what was inside. And it worked! George realized that what's on the outside doesn't always tell you what's on the inside!

But sometimes it does.

Matching Game

Match the following items to their wrappings.

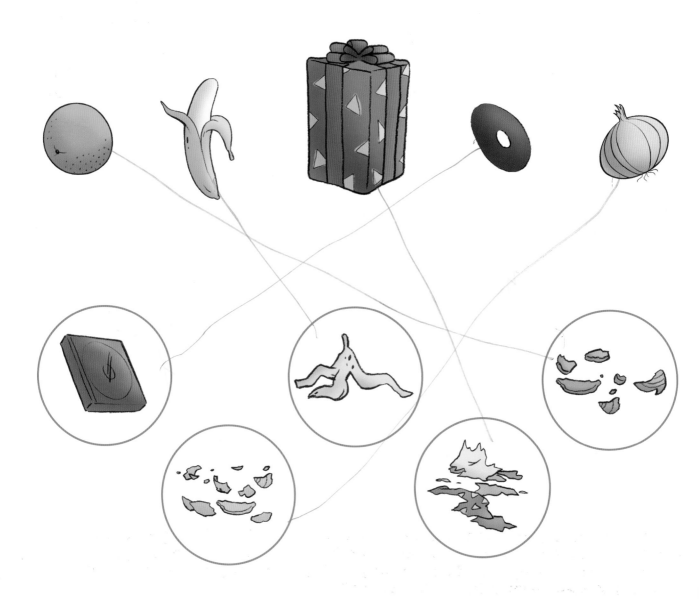

What's Inside?

For this activity you will need scissors, tape, and newspaper, wrapping paper, or old magazines. Find different-size boxes and containers in your house and put something inside. Then wrap them up! When you are finished wrapping, see if a parent or friend can guess what is inside. They can shake it, feel how heavy it is, and even ask twenty questions: Is it something I can eat? Is it bigger than a cookie? See how clues such as size and weight help you determine what you might find on the inside!

Think More About It
Can you find things in your house that are already "wrapped"? Do your favorite cookies come inside a bag? Maybe that bag is inside a box. What about your favorite cereal? And where do you keep your toys? Are they inside something else? Why do you think some things are wrapped?

Birthday Special

Draw a gift you'd like to get, and some of your favorite gifts to give:

Party Idea:
Wrap a party favor with many layers of paper (at least as many layers as the number of guests). On each layer write a funny fortune that you've come up with yourself. Each guest at your party can unwrap one layer and pass it to the next person. The person who unwraps the last layer gets to keep the prize, and everyone gets his or her fortune told!

Curious George®
Snowy Day

Adaptation by Rotem Moscovich
Based on the TV series teleplay written by Lazar Saric

George woke up to a wonderful surprise. It had snowed all night!

George was curious about all that clean, white snow. Maybe he could build something out of it.

"You go outside, George," said the man with the yellow hat. "I'll make us some cocoa for later."

This was going to be a perfect day. George went out to play. Uh-oh! He sank right into the fluffy powder!

Bill, George's friend and neighbor, came by. He did not have any trouble walking on the snow. "Hey, George," Bill said. "I have an extra pair of cross-country skis you can have."

hen Bill showed George how to ski by making
igzags through the snow. George could not
ait to try it for himself.

With skis George could stay on top of the snow, and he followed Bill uphill.
Suddenly, they heard a noise. OINK! OINK, OINK, OINK!

Bill said, "I'm going to go find out what that is. You wait here."

George waited on top of the hill in the cold. His house looked so small and warm. George wanted to get home for his cocoa. Was Bill coming back?

"Hey, George!" Bill shouted from the bottom of the hill. "I couldn't find whatever made that sound. But I have to head home now! Keep the skis and have fun!"

So George did . . . for a while.

When George was tired, he skied down the hill toward home—until he hit a rock! His skis flew off, and George tumbled the rest of the way down.

George picked himself up at the bottom of the hill. What would he do now?

He spotted two children pulling a sled. They were walking on the snow—but they did not have skis. How did they do it?

It had to be those wide flat shoes they wore.

"Vinny, I think he likes our snowshoes," the girl said.

George nodded.

"Vicky and I live on the other side of the hill," said Vinny. "If you come home with us, we'll lend you our snowshoes so you can get home too. Climb aboard the sled!"

It was fun to sail down another hill, but now George was even farther from his house.

"Here you go, monkey," Vicki said. She gave George her snowshoes and climbed on the sled. "Bye, monkey. Good luck!"

George began his long journey home. He was cold and tired, and climbing up the hill was hard work.

The thought of a nice steaming cup of cocoa kept him going.
   OINK!
   George looked up. There was that noise again. He decided to follow it.

A cold, lost pig!

What was he doing out here all by himself? And how could George rescue the poor pig?

George remembered how Vicki and Vinny had rescued him.

What George needed was a sled. It had to be flat and big enough for the pig to sit on. A fallen sign nearby looked like a good choice.

What a ride!

When George got home, he found his neighbor, Farmer Renkins, talking to the man with the yellow hat.

"Thanks for bringing my pig home, George!" the farmer said. "He got out last night before it snowed."

"Good work, George," said the man with the yellow hat. "There's some cocoa waiting for you inside."

That was exactly what George had hoped to hear.

Skiing, snowshoeing, sledding, and now cocoa . . . it had been the perfect snowy day.

SNOW SMART

George and his friends were able to travel through the deep, fluffy snow with the help of . . .

(You can circle more than one.)

AUTOMOBILE   SNOWSHOES   ROLLER SKATES   SKIS   MOTORBOAT

BOOTS   BICYCLE   SLED   ROCKET   WOODEN SIGN

DO YOU KNOW WHY?

George sank into the snow when he was wearing snow boots because he was heavier than the snowflakes underneath him. But he stayed on top of the snow when he wore skis or snowshoes because the larger area of the skis and snowshoes spread George's weight over many more snowflakes.

HELP GEORGE GET HOME!

Which track should he follow to get down the hill?

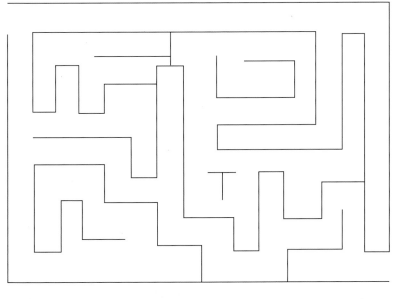

LET IT SNOW!
Make your own snowflake

Materials:
A few sheets of square paper
Safety scissors (or ask an adult for help)

INSTRUCTIONS:

1. Fold the top edge of the paper down to the bottom edge.
2. Fold the left edge over to the right edge.
3. Turn the square so that the corner with all the folds (no open edges!) is at the bottom. Fold the corner on the right side over to the left side, making a triangle.

4. Cut off the tip opposite to the fold corner. It can be pointed or rounded—experiment and see how different designs look.
5. Cut out shapes from the edges. The more shapes you cut out, the better.

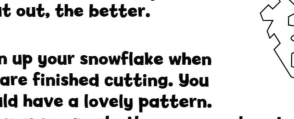

Open up your snowflake when you are finished cutting. You should have a lovely pattern.
Now you can paste it on some colored paper, put it up in your window, or hang it on a tree!

Curious George®
A Winter's Nap

Adaptation by Marcy Goldberg Sacks and Priya Giri Desai
Based on the TV series teleplay written by Craig Miller

One fall day, Bill and George went fishing. Bill saw George shivering. Maybe it was too cold to fish.

On the way home, Bill told George that some animals, such as bears, go to sleep when it gets cold.

They eat a lot in the fall. Then they hibernate, or sleep, almost all winter. George was curious. If he hibernated, he would miss the cold winter months.

At home, George ate and ate.
Maybe he would get sleepy and hibernate.

Upstairs in bed, George tried to sleep.
But his room was too bright.

George closed the curtains.
He painted a picture of the night sky.
        He still could not sleep.
How did bears do it?

George asked the man with the yellow hat about hibernation.

"This book says bears sleep in dark, quiet caves," said the man.

That was it! George needed a cave.

George hung toy bats.
He put rocks in his bed.
Now his room looked like a cave.

George settled in for his long winter nap.

Uh-oh. Now what?
George could hear sounds outside.

Pigs oinked. Cows mooed. Chickens clucked.
George shushed them, but they would not be quiet.

George covered his ears.
The animals were not as loud.
But his room was not silent yet.
George taped his blanket over the window.
Now it was dark and quiet.

Finally, George fell asleep.
He slept in his monkey cave just like a bear.

After a long time, George woke up.
He had done it!
He had hibernated.

"How did you sleep last night?" asked the man.
Last night! George had slept only one night, not all winter?
George was sad.
Then the man had an idea.
He took out a box of winter things.

The man reminded George how fun winter was. They could sled and ski together. George did not want to miss winter after all!

The Big Snooze

When animals hibernate in winter, they sleep at a time when it might be hard for them to find food. In the fall, they start to eat lots of food to store fat. Then they rest all winter long to save energy. They wake up in the spring, ready for a new season.

Bears sleep most of the winter. There are other animals that hibernate all winter long and don't wake up at all until spring.

Can you guess which animals listed include species that hibernate?

	YES	NO
BEAR	X	
LADYBUG		
CAT		
BAT		
FROG		
COW		
PIG		
GOPHER		
SQUIRREL		
SKUNK		
MONKEY		

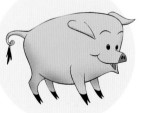

YES ANSWERS: ladybug, bat, some frogs, some gophers, some squirrels, and some skunks.

Make a Teddy Bear Cave

Put your favorite teddy bear or doll to sleep for the winter. With a few objects from inside and outside your house, you can make a cave that is comfortable to hibernate in all winter long.

1. Gather materials:
- A piece of cardboard for the floor of the cave.
- A brown paper bag to create the cave walls.
- A napkin to tuck your bear in.
- Twigs, moss, rocks, and pine needles to make the bed.
- Paints, markers, cotton balls, and anything else you need for decorating.
- A stapler.

2. Construct your cave:
- Crumple the paper bag so that you can bend it to make the cave walls and ceiling.
- With a grownup's help, staple the bag to the cardboard base. Make sure the entrance is large enough to fit your toy.
- Make the bed using the natural objects you found outside.

3. Decorate your cave like George did:
- Paint or draw bats on the cave walls.
- Place small rocks around the bed.
- Glue cotton balls around the cave to look like snow.

4. Now tuck your toy in for his own winter nap!